MR. SKINNY

by Roger Hargreaves

Mr Skinny was extraordinarily thin.

Painfully thin.

If he turned sideways, you could hardly see him at all.

And, what made it even worse, was that he lived in a place called Fatland.

Yes, Fatland!

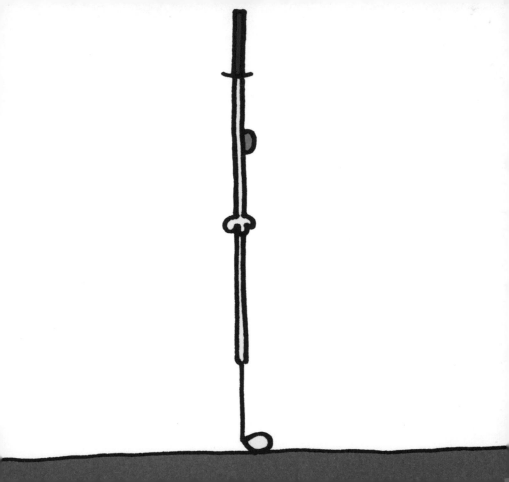

As you can very well imagine, everything and everybody in Fatland was as fat as could be.

Not stout.

Fat!

Fatland dogs were extremely fat!

Fatland worms were extraordinarily fat!

Fatland birds were exceedingly fat!

And you should see a Fatland elephant.

Phew!

And there, in the middle of all this fatness, lived Mr Skinny.

In the thinnest house you've ever seen.

Poor Mr Skinny, he didn't like being so different from everything and everybody.

But, there wasn't very much he could do about it.

You see, he had hardly any appetite at all.

A Mr Skinny meal was a very meagre affair.

Do you know what he had for breakfast?

One cornflake!

And for lunch?

One baked bean!

And for tea?

Nothing!

And for supper?

The world's smallest sausage!

And after that, he felt so full he went straight to bed.

In his long thin bed in his long thin bedroom in his long thin house, in Fatland.

"Oh, I do so wish I could do something about my appetite," he sighed to himself just before he went to sleep.

"I think," he thought, "that I had better go and see the doctor about it."

And he went to sleep.

The following morning was lovely.

A large fat sun shone down on the fat green trees and the fat yellow flowers, and through them walked Mr Skinny on his way to see the doctor.

Doctor Plump!

"Come in, come in," he wheezed as Mr Skinny knocked at his door.

"Sit down, sit down," he wheezed as Mr Skinny entered.

"And what," he wheezed, putting his plump fingers together, "seems to be the trouble?"

"It's my appetite," explained Mr Skinny. "I'd like to be able to eat more so that I could put on a little weight."

"Yes, you are rather (how shall I put it) thin," wheezed the doctor, looking at him over his glasses.

"I know," he continued, "let's start the treatment right now!"

He licked his lips.

"This very moment," he added.

And he opened a drawer in his desk and took out an enormous cream cake.

He put it on the desk in front of him.

And opened another drawer and took out half a dozen doughnuts.

And put them on the desk in front of him.

And opened another drawer and took out a dozen currant buns.

And put them on the desk in front of him.

"Elevenses," he explained.

"But it's only 10 o'clock," said Mr Skinny.

"Who's counting?" wheezed Doctor Plump.

And without further ado, he and Mr Skinny ate the lot.

Mr Skinny ate a dab of cream, a doughnut crumb and one currant.

Doctor Plump ate the rest!

"Mmm," wheezed Doctor Plump, popping the last currant bun into his mouth, and looking at Mr Skinny.

"I see," he said, "what you mean about your appetite."

He thought for a moment.

"Only one thing for it," he wheezed. "This calls for drastic measures." And he picked up his telephone in his podgy fingers and dialled a number.

One hundred miles away, the telephone rang.

PRRR PRRR! PRRR PRRR!

"Hello," said a voice.

Do you know whose voice it was?

"Mr Greedy speaking," said the voice.

Mr Greedy listened to what Doctor Plump had to say.

"You'd like a Mr Skinny to come to stay?" he said.

"To build up his appetite?" he added.

"Delighted," he agreed.

And so, Mr Skinny went to stay with Mr Greedy.

He stayed for a month.

And, during that time, Mr Greedy did manage to increase Mr Skinny's appetite.

And so, at the end of the month, Mr Skinny returned home.

Happy!

With a tummy!

A tummy was something Mr Skinny had always wanted.

"I never knew I had it in me," he chuckled to himself.

He was feeling so proud of his tummy, he decided to call in and see Doctor Plump on his way home.

"I say," wheezed Doctor Plump, looking him up and down.

"Congratulations!"

"Tell you what," he went on. "This calls for a celebration!"

And he opened his desk drawer.

Fantastic offers for Mr. Men fans!

1 MR. MEN TOKEN

Collect all your Mr. Men or Little Miss books in these superb durable collectors' cases!
Only £5.99 inc. postage and packing, these wipe-clean, hard-wearing cases will give all your Mr. Men or Little Miss books a beautiful new home!

Keep track of your collection with this giant-sized double-sided Mr. Men and Little Miss Collectors' poster.
Collect 6 tokens and we will send you a brilliant giant-sized double-sided collectors' poster! Simply tape a £1 coin to cover postage and packing in the space provided and fill out the form overleaf.

STICK £1 COIN HERE (for poster only)

Only need a few Mr. Men or Little Miss to complete your set? You can order any of the titles on the back of the books from our Mr. Men order line on 0870 787 1724. Orders should be delivered between 5 and 7 working days.

cut along the dotted line and return this whole page